THE
SCHOOL CARNIVAL
FROM THE
BLACK LAGOON

by Mike Thaler
Illustrated by Jared Lee

SCHOLASTIC INC.

New York   Toronto   London   Auckland   Sydney
Mexico City   New Delhi   Hong Kong   Buenos Aires

For little Laurel Dillon,
Welcome to the world!
—M.T.

To Kent and Jon, two clowns
—J.L.

ISBN 0-439-80075-7

Text copyright © 2005 by Mike Thaler.
Illustrations copyright © 2005 by Jared D. Lee Studio, Inc.

31 30 29 28 27 26   15 16/0

Printed in the U.S.A.
First printing, October 2005

THE
SCHOOL CARNIVAL
FROM THE
BLACK LAGOON

CONTENTS

CHAPTER 1
A BOOTH, FOR SOOTH

Our school is having a carnival. Mrs. Green says that our class has to run a booth. But what kind will it be?

She says it has to be lots of fun, easy to run, and make a ton of money! If we raise enough, we can have a real, live author come to our school. If we don't, maybe we could afford a not-so-alive author.

SCHOOL
CARNIVAL

7

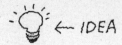 ← IDEA

Mrs. Green wants each of us to bring an idea for a carnival booth tomorrow. It is our homework for tonight. I look around at the whole class. Everyone has a blank look—this should be very interesting.

HUMM?

8

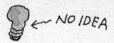
← NO IDEA

CHAPTER 2
A FAIR TO REMEMBER

On the bus ride home, we're deep in thought. We're all pretty fair-minded.

I think of all the fairs I've ever been to . . . one. It was the County Fair. It had a rodeo, and a bunch of cowboys riding bulls. Maybe I could put two horns on my dog, Tailspin.

FERRIS WHEEL

DRAGON'S NECK

ROLLER COASTER

VIKING SHIP →

LAZY SUSAN

There was also a Ferris wheel. Plus there were crazy rides, cotton candy machines, corn-dog stands, and lots more. I don't think my class can do any of that stuff.

ELEPHANT EAR

10

JELLY BEAN →

COTTON CANDY

CORN DOG →

SNOW CONE

The fair organizers gave blue ribbons to both the cows and the cabbages. I know the difference between them, but that's about all.

It's going to be a long night of homework.

CHAPTER 3
UNFAIR

When I get home, I watch a video—*My Fair Lady*. It doesn't help much. Then I listen to the weather report...fair with a chance of showers. I've got fairs on the brain. Train fares, plane fares, bus fares, pharaohs, and good fairies.

I fall asleep watching a Ferris wheel go around. Suddenly I'm at a fair. I'm walking down the midway. It has a lot of booths.

I walk up to one. It's an alligator-kissing booth. No thanks. At the next booth, I get to slam-dunk an elephant into a basketball hoop.

KISSES

Then there's a booth to bob for piranhas. If you survive that, you get to wrestle a bear. There are also booths for throwing marshmallows at balloons and for floating feathers in milk bottles. So far, I have not won anything.

GRRRR

14

Suddenly I'm in a gigantic fish bowl. Kids are trying to win me. They're throwing ping-pong balls that are bouncing all around. This is not fun. So I climb out of the bowl and go to buy a hotdog. But it's Tailspin in a bun.

MARS

PING!
PING!
PING!

PING-PONG BALLS →

HOT DOG ↙

15

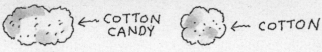

Then I buy some cotton candy, but it's made of real cotton. I wake up and see that I'm chewing on my pillow.

16

CHAPTER 4
MIRROR, MIRROR ON THE WALL . . .

On the school bus, everyone is excited. I think that they all have ideas, but no one's telling. They're waiting for class.

"Alright," says Mrs. Green. "Who has an idea for our class booth?"

Every hand shoots up. Penny raises two.

"Do you have an idea, Penny?"

"A kissing booth!" puckers Penny.

"YUCK! That won't make too much money," says Eric. "And besides, it's unsanitary!"

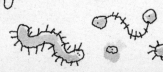

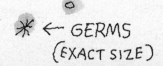

← GERMS
(EXACT SIZE)

17

Mrs. Green calls on Freddy.

"A bakery booth. I'll bake a lot of apple turnovers, and we'll sell them. We'll have a fast turnover," jokes Freddy.

"Possible," says Mrs. Green.

"Let's have a cakewalk," says Derrick.

"Great," says Freddy. "Then I'll bake a cake."

MEET THE COOK ←

I LOVE APPLES.

APPLE TURNOVERS

WORM BOY →

Eric waves his hand. "I'll get a crystal ball and tell the future."

"You can't tell the future," sneers Doris.

"I knew you would say that," smiles Eric.

CATERPILLAR CHIC

PAPER BALL → ○ GOLF BALL → ○ RUBBER BALL → ○ EYE-BALL → ○

"What about a basketball shoot?" says Randy.

"No way," says Eric. "Those fifth graders are too good, and they'll win all of our prizes."

"We could shoot meatballs instead," says Freddy.

HANDMADE PAPER BALLS →

"Too messy," I say. "What about a dunking tank?"

There's silence in the room. Mrs. Green turns and writes all the ideas on the board.

KISSING BOOTH
BAKERY BOOTH
CAKEWALK
FORTUNE-TELLER
BASKETBALL SHOOT
DUNKING TANK

SUGGESTION BOX

"Let's vote," she says.

The dunking tank idea wins hands down—or hands up.

"But who will we dunk?" asks Mrs. Green.

Everyone looks at her.

"No way!" says Mrs. Green.

ANY VOLUNTEERS?

Then everyone looks at me.

"I catch colds so easily," I announce. "What about dunking doughnuts?"

"I could bake the doughnuts," says Freddy.

"It was your idea," says Penny.

"Scared?" sneers Eric.

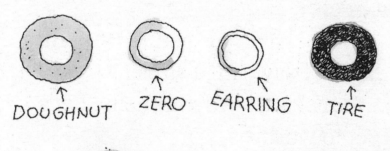

↑
DOUGHNUT ZERO EARRING TIRE

WHAT?

23

I notice that everyone's staring at me.

"Me scared?" I squeak. "Not a chance."

"Then you will do it," says Eric.

"On one condition," I say.

"What's that?" asks Mrs. Green.

"You have to use ping-pong balls," I say with a smile.

"OK," says Mrs. Green. "Let's get to work."

WHAT NOISE DOES A MOUSE MAKE?
(CIRCLE ONE)

1. ROAR
2. SQUEAK
3. TWEET

ANSWER ON PAGE 30

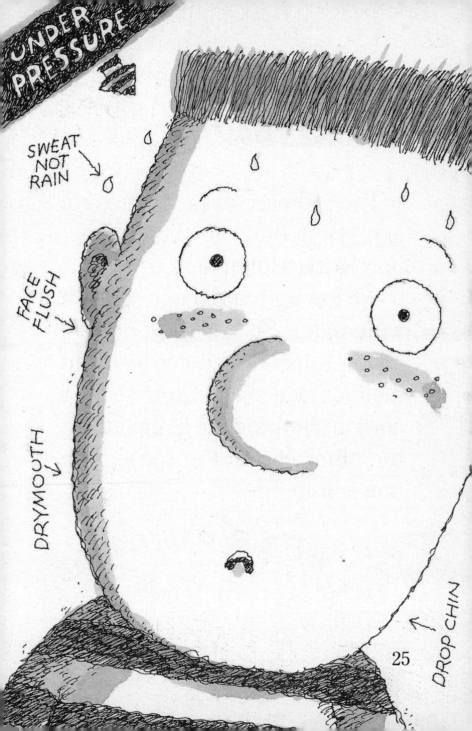

CHAPTER 5
THE BETTER MOUSETRAP

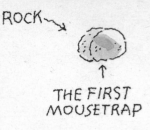

ROCK →

THE FIRST MOUSETRAP

The whole class pitches in and starts building the dunking booth. It's a lot of fun!

We get a plastic pool and fill it with water. So far, so good. We attach a chair to a hinged platform held up by a stick. Then we tie a cord around the stick and attach the other end to the spring of a mousetrap. Bingo!

"BINGO" IS THE NAME OF:
(CIRCLE ONE)

1. A LITTLE CAR
2. A GAME
3. A LARGE BIRD

ANSWER ON PAGE 35

26

We hit the trap. The spring snaps forward. It jerks the rope that pulls the stick, which drops the platform, and whoever is sitting in the chair falls into the water. *Splash!*

THE DUNKEE

① PING-PONG BALL

② STRING

③

④

⑤

STICK

HINGE

DON'T FORGET TO ADD WATER.

Hey, that'll be me. I'll be dropping into the water. Oh, me and my bright ideas! I don't even know how to swim. I better learn . . . fast.

SHARK

SNACK

CHAPTER 6
AQUA-PHOBIA!

I've always been afraid of the water. I'd rather stand on land than sink in the drink. It's fine for fish, but it's not my wish. But now, I have to learn how to swim.

My mom signs me up and takes me down to the public swimming pool. It's big! And it's full of water! It's six feet deep. Maybe I should go home and grow. I'll come back when I'm eight feet tall.

6 — - - - - 6 FEET

5

4

3 — - - - 3 FEET (ALMOST)

2

1

A nice lady comes over. She's got a whistle and a clipboard.

"I'm Miss Titanic, your swim instructor," she says.

"I want to miss this *Titanic*," I mutter.

"What?" she asks.

"Uh, nice to meet you, Miss Titanic," I reply.

QUACK.

"You must be Hubie," she says with a smile.

"Do I have to be?" I answer.

"You're right on time for your lesson," she says, checking her clipboard.

"Can I wait a couple of years?" I ask.

"Are we a little afraid of the water?" she laughs.

"Not if it's in a cup," I say.

"Just pretend that the pool is a big cup," she replies.

"I'm not that thirsty," I say, as she puts water wings on each of my arms.

"Let's start off in the shallow end," she says, taking my hand.

"Any puddle is fine," I say.

"Come on, Hubie." She leads me down the steps into the pool. The water is very wet.

TOWELS

"Now duck, Hubie," she says.

"Quack, quack."

"No. Duck down," she laughs.

I shut my eyes, hold my breath, and duck down.

Phew! Waaaf! Schlurp!

"Now was that so bad?" she asks.

"Actually, it wasn't," I sigh.

"Now duck and open your eyes under the water."

"My eyeballs will drown," I protest.

"No, they won't. First, take a deep breath and hold it."

WOW!

35

ANSWER: A GAME

I keep my eyes open and they don't drown. I can actually see underwater. Maybe I have X-ray vision. I feel like a superhero... POOLMAN!

Anyway, in my first lesson I also learn to float. I'm a good floater. Maybe one day I can win an Olympic gold medal in floating. But more important, I'm almost ready for the carnival.

CHAPTER 7
FAIR-WEATHER FRIENDS

The whole school yard is alive with activity. Each class is putting up a booth. There's a ring toss, a baseball pitch, a basketball throw, a Frisbee fling, a tiddlywinks flip, and a lob the blob. There's even a turtle race. Why didn't I think of that?

37

There's a wheel of fortune, a fortune-teller, and a telescope. You can see the future for a dollar, or the full moon for fifty cents, or a quarter moon for a quarter.

There's going to be a pie-eating contest. Freddy will probably win that. There's also a jelly bean contest. If you guess the number of jelly beans in a big jar, you can win a pair of Rollerblades.

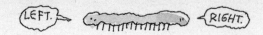

"Every booth has a name," says Mrs. Green. "So what's the name of ours?"

"What about Dip the Drip?" replies Penny.

The rest of the class keeps on yelling out names.

"Spill the Pill," giggles Doris.

"Wet the Pet," grins Randy.

"Drown the Clown," laughs Derrick.

"Hey, that's me you're talking about!" I shout.

40

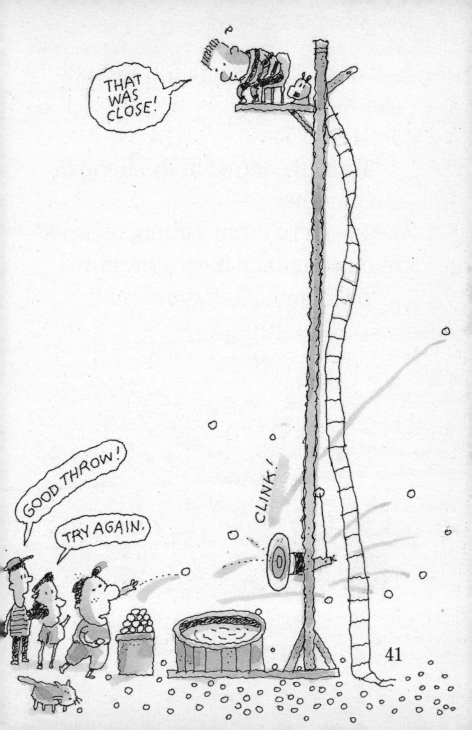

41

"What about Dunk the Skunk!" laughs Freddy.

"Hey!" I say.

"Dunk the Punk!" they all shout out together.

"I have it," I say, putting on my water wings and flexing my arms. "What about Dunk the Hunk!"

CHAPTER 8

IN THE SWIM

Well, it's Friday. The carnival is tonight. Are people that go to carnivals called *carnivores*? Everyone's very excited to see the Daredevil Diver. That's me. But it's more like the Dubious Diver.

A CARNIVORE IS:

1. A MEAT-EATER.
2. A CAR THAT RUNS ON GARLIC.
3. A TREE THAT GROWS IN WISCONSIN.

ANSWER ON PAGE 49

43

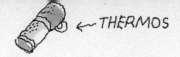

COLD
FEET →

← THERMOS

I must admit that I'm getting cold feet. It could be very chilly tonight. The water could be freezing. I could get *hypo-thermos* or frostbite.

ICE

I go into the principal's office and ask Mr. Bender if he'll sit in for me. He says that he won't because at the County Fair he got hit with a pie during a charity event.

For the rest of the day, kids are wisecracking jokes at me.

"Taking the big plunge tonight, eh, Hubie?"

"You'll be a titanic success," someone chimes in.

"You'll make a big splash tonight!" another kid laughs.

They're getting me down in the dumps. I have fair-weather friends.

I'm not ready for this!

I need six more years of swimming lessons.

"And besides, Hubie, you're the original hunk!" a bunch of kids yell.

That's funny because I feel more like the original junk.

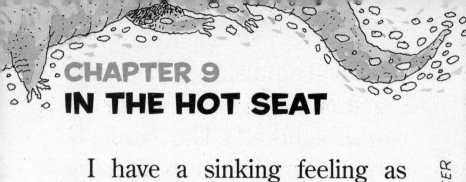

CHAPTER 9
IN THE HOT SEAT

I have a sinking feeling as the carnival draws near. Mom drives me to school in the van. I'm taking 42 towels. I bought a fluorescent bathing suit so the rescue helicopter can spot me in the water. And I have three sets of water wings.

ANSWER: A MEAT-EATER

WOP WOP

WOP WOP WOP

THERE HE IS.

OVER HERE!

DROP THE HUNK ROPE.

We pull right up to the carnival. I step out of the van and into a row of lights. It's like Academy Award night. I slowly walk down the aisle. All eyes are on me. I come to our booth, which we finally named, "The Big Dipper."

I take off my bathrobe, put on my three sets of water wings, flex, and climb the ladder to the chair. It's high up here. I'm *fair-in-height*.

HOT SEAT →

THE CHEERS HAVE STOPPED.

DEAD SILENCE FALLS OVER THE CROWD.

51

I can see over most of the carnival.

Penny's selling tickets like crazy. Freddy's eating pie. And Randy's counting jelly beans. There are a lot of people in a long line, looking up to see me drown.

All my friends are at the front of the line. Eric is the first to try. He misses the mousetrap completely.

ONE, PLEASE.

TICKETS

DRAT!

DON'T CROSS THAT LINE.

MEOW.

GRRRR.

52

53

Derek and Doris get closer, but I am still high and dry. Freddy tries with blueberry pie all over his face. He misses, too.

Then the rest of the third grade takes a shot. I was smart to use ping-pong balls.

The tension mounts as ball after ball bounces off the trap, but each is too light to spring it. I make it through the fourth and fifth graders.

We're making a fortune and I'm still a dry guy in the sky!

CHAPTER 10
THE SLAM DUNK

Now the teachers start trying to sink me. Miss La Note, my music teacher, sings and misses.

Then Miss Swamp, my art teacher, draws a blank when she throws.

Even, Ms. Pluggins, the new computer teacher, takes a shot and short-circuits.

Finally, Mr. Bender buys a chance. I think he remembered that I was the guy who hit him with the pie at the County Fair! He misses, too. PHEW!

57

I'm feeling really good. I've beat the system. No one is in line anymore. I do a little victory dance on my chair.

I have a big, dry smile. Just as I am getting ready to climb down, I see something moving by the mousetrap.

Oh, no! A mouse!

INTERESTING.

The little rodent puts one foot on the trap and —WHAM! I'm in the water, and so is the mouse! He's a pretty good swimmer.

The water is not so cold. In fact, it's kind of fun. Everyone applauds as the mouse and I swim around.

We're the hit of the school carnival and even get our picture taken for the paper. I hope we're on the front page. The headline will probably read: BIG AND LITTLE DIPPERS.

WHAT FOOD DO MICE LOVE THE MOST?

1. WATERMELON
2. CHEESE
3. JELLY BEANS

MENU

ANSWER ON PAGE 63

CIRCLE THE
CANNONBALL →   ○

Well, I continue with my swimming lessons. Last Friday, I did a cannonball off the diving board. I haven't seen the mouse at the pool, though. I think he went to the Mouse Olympics in Mouse-cow. Hey, maybe one day I'll win a gold medal, too.

LOOK OF CONFIDENCE.
↓

FIRST AID
KIT JUST
IN CASE.
↓

As it turns out, Randy's guess was the closest to the number of jelly beans and he won the Rollerblades. Freddy won the eating contest. He said it was as easy as pie. And we ended up raising enough money to get a fairly well-known author to come and visit our school.

GAINED 10 POUNDS

COOK

TOMORROW IS AUTHOR DAY
BRING MONEY TO BUY HIS BOOKS

COOL.

AWESOME!

I'M BRINGING A CAMERA.

63